序言

自 103 年起，正式實施十二年國教，對國中生來說，最重要的轉變，就是取代國中基測的「國中教育會考」。會考難度大於以往的基測，因此，平常就要不斷地練習，到眞正考試時，才能獲得高分。

「會考單字文法考前 *660* 題題本」總共收錄了六十六回測驗，每一回測驗有十題，在這十道題目中，題型完全仿照會考，隨機出題，讓同學有臨場測驗的感受。出題範圍限於國中常用 1200 字，讓同學充分複習會考常考字彙。

「會考單字文法考前 *660* 題題本」特別針對想要在考試前增強解題速度和準確度的學生編寫，題目較「會考單字文法 *500* 題題本」複雜困難。內容多元且生活化，符合一般生活的情境，同學可以在練習完 500 題後，馬上自我挑戰再寫 660 題，一定能在會考拿下最好的分數。

如果想把英文考好，有個觀念要謹記在心，那就是「單字非常重要」，不管你是要寫單字文法題、克漏字，還是閱讀測驗，如果大部分的單字都看不懂，根本不可能拿高分。所以無論如何，一定要花時間、下功夫，把該背的單字背下來，然後再做題目練習，確實了解關鍵字彙的用法，這就是英文考高分的方法。方法很簡單，只要肯努力，就會成功。

本書另附有「教師手冊」，每一題都有答案、翻譯，和清楚的文法解釋，完全解除同學們的疑惑。

書在編審及校對的每一階段，均力求完善，但恐有疏漏之處，誠盼各界先進不吝批評指正。

編者 謹識

TEST · 1

※下列各題，請依文意選出一個最適當的答案。

1. School begins in September after a long ________ vacation.
   (A) superman
   (B) summer
   (C) sweater
   (D) swimming ( )

2. Of all the novels, which do you like ________?
   (A) better
   (B) best
   (C) more
   (D) much ( )

3. My father and I cleaned the rooms ________.
   (A) himself
   (B) ourself
   (C) ourselves
   (D) myself ( )

4. Tony has to mop the floor, ________ he?
   (A) has
   (B) mustn't
   (C) does
   (D) doesn't ( )

5. Most American western movies are about ________.
   (A) cram schools
   (B) cowboys
   (C) classmates
   (D) colors ( )

6. Mrs. Carter enjoys watching her husband __________ dinner.
   (A) cooks
   (B) cooking
   (C) to cook
   (D) cooked ( )

7. I broke my mother's vase. She was a little angry and told me not to do it __________.
   (A) carefully
   (B) along
   (C) again
   (D) before ( )

8. We need __________ when we make a call, take the bus, and get a Coke from a vending machine.
   (A) cheap
   (B) child
   (C) change
   (D) clean ( )

9. The Lin family have lived in Taipei __________ twenty years, haven't they?
   (A) for
   (B) since
   (C) when
   (D) in ( )

10. __________ was fun to play basketball with your brothers last week.
   (A) It
   (B) That
   (C) This
   (D) There ( )

TEST · 2

※ 下列各題，請依文意選出一個最適當的答案。

1. Susan goes to __________ with her family almost every Sunday morning.
   (A) church
   (B) catch
   (C) control
   (D) closet ( )

2. Eating green vegetables __________ good for health.
   (A) is
   (B) has
   (C) are
   (D) have ( )

3. Remember __________ your uncle if you go to New York.
   (A) visiting
   (B) to visit
   (C) call on
   (D) calling ( )

4. Every morning, there is a vendor selling rice balls on the __________.
   (A) country
   (B) cover
   (C) cookie
   (D) corner ( )

5. Don't waste so much time __________ comic books.
   (A) watching
   (B) read
   (C) reading
   (D) studying ( )

6. A __________ is a part of the city. There are usually four streets around it.
   (A) bookstore
   (B) clock
   (C) village
   (D) block ( )

7. We should learn English not only because it's a school subject __________ because it's useful and interesting.
   (A) from
   (B) then
   (C) also
   (D) but ( )

8. We had to wait in a long line to get a __________ when we went to a movie in the past, but now we can do that at home on the computer.
   (A) card
   (B) menu
   (C) ticket
   (D) theater ( )

9. The tickets to the baseball game __________ out in two days, won't they?
   (A) is going to be sold
   (B) are sold
   (C) will be sold
   (D) won't sell ( )

10. The baseball game __________ the Dinos and the Elephants was very exciting.
   (A) believe
   (B) beside
   (C) because
   (D) between ( )

TEST · 3

※下列各題，請依文意選出一個最適當的答案。

1. The subject is ________, and I am ________.
   (A) confused ; troubled
   (B) confused ; troubling
   (C) confusing ; troubled
   (D) confusing ; troubling ( )

2. My older sister is a good cook. She usually cooks ________ food for our family.
   (A) delicious
   (B) decorate
   (C) dessert
   (D) decide ( )

3. ________, I'll watch that TV program at home.
   (A) If it were raining tomorrow
   (B) If it will rain tomorrow
   (C) If it rained tomorrow
   (D) If it rains tomorrow ( )

4. Mary had to stay at home ________.
   (A) since she caught a bad cold
   (B) she was also given a lot of work
   (C) that she was given something hard to do
   (D) she did much homework, too ( )

5. ________ has the least days of all the twelve months.
   (A) December
   (B) February
   (C) March
   (D) August ( )

6. It's usually hard for me to make a _________ when I am in a Chinese restaurant.
   (A) dialogue
   (B) difference
   (C) difficulty
   (D) decision ( )

7. I hope one day I will _________ create a new language.
   (A) may
   (B) can
   (C) be able to
   (D) able to ( )

8. We usually say, "_________," when we want to ask someone a question, or when we ask someone for help.
   (A) I'm sorry
   (B) Excuse me
   (C) You're welcome
   (D) Not at all ( )

9. My mother gave me an English _________ and it helps me a lot when I read English novels.
   (A) dictionary
   (B) notebook
   (C) teacher
   (D) gold ( )

10. Lots of things _________ since I last wrote to you.
    (A) happened
    (B) were happened
    (C) have happened
    (D) have been happened ( )

TEST · 4

※ 下列各題，請依文意選出一個最適當的答案。

1. We use a(n) ________ when we mail a letter to someone, and we have to write the receiver's name and address on it.
   (A) machine
   (B) pen friend
   (C) envelope
   (D) e-mail ( )

   receiver 收信人

2. Do you remember ________?
   (A) where is it
   (B) when she will come
   (C) who should you see
   (D) how could this happen ( )

3. I usually watch movies on TV because movie tickets are too ________.
   (A) example
   (B) experience
   (C) expensive
   (D) exercise ( )

4. Our school bus ________ at seven-thirty every morning.
   (A) to start
   (B) starts
   (C) starting
   (D) will start ( )

5. If I ________ money, I would lend it to you.
   (A) had
   (B) have had
   (C) have
   (D) could have ( )

6. John likes sports, but I like reading. My interest is __________ from his.
   (A) familiar
   (B) the same
   (C) similar
   (D) different ( )

7. During the typhoon season, the __________ are often delayed. So before you go to the airport, you have to make a call to know if yours has been delayed.
   (A) sky
   (B) flights
   (C) magazines
   (D) light ( )

8. A customer's order might be ready so quickly __________.
   (A) after he left right away
   (B) that he could leave right after paying for it
   (C) if he would not like to pay for it
   (D) since he began to wait ( )

9. We often say, "__________," when someone is going to take a test.
   (A) Have a nice trip
   (B) Good luck
   (C) Take care
   (D) Mind your own business ( )

10. Our English teacher usually told us to write down her words in our __________.
   (A) notebooks
   (B) museums
   (C) homework
   (D) newspapers ( )

TEST · 5

※ 下列各題，請依文意選出一個最適當的答案。

1. My grandmother said that cows work hard on the farm for us, so we shouldn't eat ________.
   (A) beef
   (B) pork
   (C) chicken
   (D) fish ( )

2. He especially loves ________ with his father.
   (A) go to fish
   (B) go to fishing
   (C) to go to fishing
   (D) to go fishing ( )

3. The day which you were born on is your ________.
   (A) present
   (B) holiday
   (C) everyday
   (D) birthday ( )

4. Which sentence is **wrong**?
   (A) Mary will be here soon, <u>won't she</u>?
   (B) It's a nice day, <u>isn't it</u>?
   (C) You don't know where Karen is, <u>do you</u>?
   (D) She's got beautiful eyes, <u>isn't she</u>? ( )

5. Tina is busy ________ her new house.
   (A) decorating
   (B) to decorate
   (C) for decorating
   (D) decorate ( )

6. Doctors write prescriptions for the sick people to get some __________ in the hospital.
   (A) money
   (B) nurse
   (C) medicine
   (D) medium ( )

7. __________ is the name of a city in Germany, but in English it means a kind of fast food.
   (A) French fries
   (B) Sandwich
   (C) Hamburg
   (D) Nugget ( )

8. My sister likes to put __________ of movie stars and singers on the wall in her room.
   (A) clock
   (B) names
   (C) fans
   (D) posters ( )

9. __________ you stay in bed for a few days, you will get better.
   (A) Even if
   (B) Although
   (C) That
   (D) As long as ( )

10. I love __________ most because Christmas is in that month and I can get a lot of presents and cards.
   (A) August
   (B) September
   (C) December
   (D) October ( )

TEST · 6

※下列各題，請依文意選出一個最適當的答案。

1. A：What languages can you ______?
   B：Mandarin, Taiwanese, and a little English.
   (A) say
   (B) talk
   (C) tell
   (D) speak ( )

2. We Chinese live on ______.
   (A) bread
   (B) lunch
   (C) dinner
   (D) rice ( )

3. I call my mother ______ a week.
   (A) twice
   (B) town
   (C) twin
   (D) truth ( )

4. ______ is not very difficult.
   (A) Ride a bicycle
   (B) A new subject becomes confusing
   (C) Correct studying habits
   (D) Remembering facts ( )

5. The police ______ the thief.
   (A) has caught
   (B) have caught
   (C) have catched
   (D) has catched ( )

6. Susan __________ has dessert after meals because she is afraid of getting fat.
   (A) always
   (B) usually
   (C) often
   (D) seldom ( )

7. The day which comes before Thursday and after Tuesday is __________.
   (A) Sunday
   (B) Saturday
   (C) Wednesday
   (D) Friday ( )

8. If you go to Hualien by __________ from Taipei, it will take you about four hours.
   (A) plane
   (B) train
   (C) bike
   (D) boat ( )

9. One day you found your shoes were too small. It meant that your __________ had gotten bigger.
   (A) feet
   (B) legs
   (C) fingers
   (D) hair ( )

10. During summer vacation, some students go __________ about nature.
   (A) camping and learned
   (B) camping and learn
   (C) camp and learn
   (D) to camp and to be learned ( )

TEST · 7

※下列各題，請依文意選出一個最適當的答案。

1. If you want to go outdoors and relax, you can go bird watching in the ________ or go swimming in the ocean.
   (A) mountains
   (B) movies
   (C) music
   (D) museums ( )

2. ________ are two hamburgers and one Coke?
   (A) How much
   (B) How many dollar
   (C) How much dollars
   (D) How many money ( )

3. My boyfriend bought a new dress ________ me.
   (A) to
   (B) of
   (C) ×
   (D) for ( )

4. I don't know ________
   (A) how to fix a bike.
   (B) where is he going.
   (C) what is he going to do?
   (D) when he to leave. ( )

5. Don't play ball on the ________.
   (A) steak
   (B) luck
   (C) farm
   (D) road ( )

6. Mother prepares food for us in the ________.
   (A) kitchen
   (B) supermarket
   (C) restaurant
   (D) living room ( )

7. My mother had to work last night, so she left a note on the table. It ________, "Remember to lock the door before going to bed."
   (A) told
   (B) wrote
   (C) spoke
   (D) said ( )

8. Tom didn't study hard during his last two junior high school years. Now he is ________ about the coming Comprehensive Assessment Program for Junior High School Students.
   (A) confused
   (B) worried
   (C) bored
   (D) excited ( )

9. ________ hard, and you will have a great success.
   (A) If you work
   (B) To work
   (C) Working
   (D) Work ( )

10. Last Saturday I went to the night market with my classmates. I bought some CDs from a ________, and they were cheaper there.
    (A) visitor
    (B) voice
    (C) video
    (D) vendor ( )

TEST · 8

※下列各題，請依文意選出一個最適當的答案。

1. Susan is getting fatter and fatter. So she goes to the gym to get __________ almost every day.
   (A) hamburger
   (B) exercise
   (C) experience
   (D) example　　　　(　)

2. "You're never too old to __________," is an old saying.
   (A) teach
   (B) learn
   (C) talk
   (D) get　　　　(　)

3. Suddenly, he saw a man __________ at the corner.
   (A) standing
   (B) stands
   (C) to stand
   (D) who stand　　　　(　)

4. They must stay in the house __________.
   (A) if they are convenient
   (B) where Mr. Lin owns
   (C) because it's raining
   (D) and I am, too　　　　(　)

5. Can you go traveling alone without __________?
   (A) to lose
   (B) losing
   (C) lost
   (D) getting lost　　　　(　)

6. Tom : What time can we have dinner, Mom?
   Mom : __________
   (A) Pretty soon.
   (B) Not now.
   (C) Not yet.
   (D) Don't you know? ( )

7. "It rained cats and dogs last night," means we had a __________ rain last night.
   (A) handy
   (B) hardly
   (C) heavy
   (D) heavily ( )

8. "__________" can be used both when we answer the telephone and when we meet someone.
   (A) Hi!
   (B) Hello.
   (C) How are you?
   (D) Nice to meet you. ( )

9. John did not __________ to school yesterday.
   He __________ to school.
   (A) walked ; ran
   (B) walk ; run
   (C) walk ; ran
   (D) walked ; run ( )

10. __________ are very warm-hearted people. They volunteer to help old people in town.
    (A) The Anderson's family
    (B) The Anderson
    (C) The Andersons
    (D) Anderson family ( )

TEST · 9

※下列各題，請依文意選出一個最適當的答案。

1. I have never ________ a fire ________ matches.
   (A) starting ; with
   (B) began ; by
   (C) started ; with
   (D) beginning ; by ( )

2. This is ________ and I hope you like it.
   (A) a house of my
   (B) my own house
   (C) house for my own
   (D) a my own house ( )

3. The stories ________ by Mr. Wang are quite interesting.
   (A) were written
   (B) are written
   (C) written
   (D) wrote ( )

4. My mother had me ________ before dinner.
   (A) finish reading the book
   (B) finish to read the book
   (C) to finish to read the book
   (D) finishing reading the book ( )

5. "________" means the weather is neither cold nor hot, but now it also means "in fashion" to the young people.
   (A) Cool
   (B) Nice
   (C) Warm
   (D) Cute ( )

6. Frank's grandmother can't read without wearing her __________.
   (A) watch
   (B) jacket
   (C) glasses
   (D) dress ( )

7. Children are happier during the Chinese New Year because they can get lucky money from __________.
   (A) red envelopes
   (B) grownups
   (C) banks
   (D) clerks ( )

8. My books are on the desk. Those in the box __________.
   (A) is yours
   (B) is my sisters'
   (C) are her
   (D) are his ( )

9. Lily __________ one hour playing the piano almost every day.
   (A) takes
   (B) spends
   (C) costs
   (D) haves ( )

10. When you drop your spoon at the restaurant, you don't have to pick it up and use it. You can ask the __________ for another one.
    (A) water
    (B) waste
    (C) waiter
    (D) wallet ( )

TEST · 10

※下列各題，請依文意選出一個最適當的答案。

1. Susan always ________ table tennis after school.
   (A) tries
   (B) listens to
   (C) practices
   (D) follows ( )

2. Women's sweaters may be ________.
   (A) more expensive than men's
   (B) more expensive than mens'
   (C) much expensive than mens'
   (D) very expensive than mans' ( )

3. How about ________?
   (A) we growing rice
   (B) go on a picnic
   (C) playing volleyball
   (D) to join some winter programs ( )

4. He is too young ________.
   (A) to driving
   (B) can't drive
   (C) that can't drive
   (D) to drive ( )

5. Tom talked about his problems ________.
   (A) sad as Jack
   (B) Jack as sadly
   (C) as sad as Jack
   (D) as sadly as Jack ( )

6. When I have problems in learning English, my teacher always gives me some good ________ to follow.
   (A) songs
   (B) novels
   (C) answers
   (D) tips ( )

7. During Chinese New Year, people like to ________ their relatives or friends to come to their houses to get together.
   (A) invite
   (B) return
   (C) compete
   (D) spend ( )

8. Some people enjoy taking the MRT because the MRT is more ________ than the bus.
   (A) comfortable
   (B) strong
   (C) expensive
   (D) shy ( )

9. My sister is a big fan of "Mayday." She goes to ________ every concert.
   (A) surely
   (B) almost
   (C) ever
   (D) mostly ( )

10. The weather report says there ________ some rain tomorrow.
   (A) will have
   (B) has
   (C) will be
   (D) is ( )

TEST · 11

※下列各題，請依文意選出一個最適當的答案。

1. A good driver has to drive ________.
   (A) differently
   (B) carefully
   (C) specially
   (D) actively ( )

2. Jack is never late for school. ________
   (A) Neither do I.
   (B) Neither am I.
   (C) Either do I.
   (D) Either am I. ( )

3. My friend said that Australia is a nice country to ________.
   (A) visit
   (B) join
   (C) think
   (D) pay ( )

4. Aesop's fables are animal stories ________ important lessons to people.
   (A) which teach
   (B) which teaches
   (C) who teach
   (D) who teaches ( )

5. Tom was ________ when I called.
   (A) having dinner
   (B) bake a cake
   (C) painted the walls
   (D) had the dinner ( )

6. My teacher told me that if I wanted to be a doctor, I needed to study medical ________.
   (A) science
   (B) novels
   (C) music
   (D) sports ( )

7. Be ________ to tell your parents when you're going to come home late; otherwise, they will be very worried about you.
   (A) huge
   (B) fresh
   (C) sure
   (D) easy ( )

8. I would like Bill ________.
   (A) learn a new language
   (B) to come right away
   (C) busy a good book
   (D) teaching my brother ( )

9. The house ________ Helen moved into is not far from our school.
   (A) here
   (B) there
   (C) which
   (D) it ( )

10. Last night, David fell into a hole on his way home. It was a(n) ________ experience.
    (A) embarrassed
    (B) excited
    (C) embarrassing
    (D) exciting ( )

TEST · 12

※下列各題，請依文意選出一個最適當的答案。

1. I am used to drinking ________ after each meal.
   (A) seafood
   (B) tea
   (C) vegetable
   (D) fruit ( )

2. The book was ________ that I ________ put it down.
   (A) so good ; can
   (B) so well ; can't
   (C) so good ; couldn't
   (D) so well ; could ( )

3. One of the tips for being a good learner is to ________ the new lesson before class.
   (A) review
   (B) own
   (C) preview
   (D) wake ( )

4. If I were tired, ________.
   (A) I'll go to bed earlier
   (B) I'd stop taking a rest
   (C) I would be full of energy
   (D) I'd go for a walk ( )

5. One of my hands is clean, but ________ isn't.
   (A) the other
   (B) another
   (C) each other
   (D) other ( )

6. Could you tell me where I can buy a new ________?
I lost mine at the movie theater last night.
(A) paint
(B) wallet
(C) credit card
(D) nap ( )

7. If I study harder, I believe I will get ________ grades on my tests.
(A) better
(B) worse
(C) best
(D) worst ( )

8. This morning, Mom asked me to buy a ________ of bread at the bakery.
(A) loaf
(B) glass
(C) carton
(D) can ( )

9. The prize that everybody wished to get ________ to John finally.
(A) went
(B) going
(C) to go
(D) go ( )

10. Cathy always ________ listening to an English radio station before she goes to bed.
(A) wants to
(B) needs to
(C) enjoys
(D) has to ( )

TEST · 13

※下列各題，請依文意選出一個最適當的答案。

1. It’s not difficult to learn a language as long as you __________ your studies.
   (A) come on
   (B) wait on
   (C) call on
   (D) concentrate on ( )

2. On his last trip to New York, __________
   (A) something interesting was happened to him.
   (B) interesting something happened to him.
   (C) something interesting happened to him.
   (D) he happened something interesting. ( )

3. I just ran __________ coffee. I am going to get some later.
   (A) by
   (B) after
   (C) into
   (D) out of ( )

4. Rebecca’s husband __________ for ten years.
   (A) has been dead
   (B) has died
   (C) died
   (D) was dead ( )

5. Mr. Lin, __________, will take us to the zoo tomorrow.
   (A) is our English teacher
   (B) that is our English teacher
   (C) our English teacher
   (D) who and our English teacher ( )

6. Most people like ________ because they don't have to go to school or go to work. They can just relax.
   (A) churches
   (B) envelopes
   (C) weekends
   (D) experiences ( )

7. When my brother studied in New Zealand, he enjoyed reading English ________ in his free time.
   (A) courts
   (B) questions
   (C) envelopes
   (D) novels ( )

8. Many passengers forgot to take their things when they ________ the MRT.
   (A) got on
   (B) got off
   (C) got in
   (D) got out of ( )

9. She is an ________ person. We all enjoy ________ to her.
   (A) interesting ; talking
   (B) interesting ; talk
   (C) interest ; talking
   (D) interested ; to talk ( )

10. Mary is not interested in playing baseball. She always gets ________ it.
   (A) bored with
   (B) active in
   (C) excited by
   (D) satisfied with ( )

TEST · 14

※ 下列各題，請依文意選出一個最適當的答案。

1. Playing computer games ________ a lot of young students.
   (A) interest
   (B) interests
   (C) is interested in
   (D) are interesting to ( )

2. I don't know ________.
   (A) what to do
   (B) how to do
   (C) where is she
   (D) when did he leave ( )

3. Turning left here is ________, so we have to keep going along the street.
   (A) fast
   (B) helpful
   (C) illegal
   (D) useful ( )

4. I asked the foreigner ________ she could speak Chinese.
   (A) that
   (B) if
   (C) what
   (D) which ( )

5. It's very important. Please ________ to this carefully.
   (A) watch
   (B) listen
   (C) feel
   (D) hear ( )

6. A : __________ to Hong Kong?
   B : No, but I'd like to. I hear it's very nice.
   (A) Have you been
   (B) Were you going
   (C) Have you gone
   (D) Do you go ( )

7. Do you think it's more difficult to learn math __________ English?
   (A) while
   (B) than
   (C) then
   (D) that ( )

8. I am __________ to visit many places in Australia with my best friend next winter.
   (A) planning
   (B) catching
   (C) walking
   (D) playing ( )

9. Everyone knows that there are sixty __________ in an hour, and twenty-four hours in a day.
   (A) minutes
   (B) seconds
   (C) museums
   (D) colors ( )

10. When my family has __________ time, we like to go swimming together.
   (A) free
   (B) special
   (C) different
   (D) busy ( )

TEST · 15

※下列各題，請依文意選出一個最適當的答案。

1. ________ I work with are very ________.
   (A) One of the persons ; quickly
   (B) Some of the people ; friendly
   (C) Some of the peoples ; carefully
   (D) All of the people ; strangely ( )

2. My watch is not running. I want to buy ________.
   (A) the other one
   (B) another one
   (C) it
   (D) other one ( )

3. Donna decided ________ my younger brother, Ben.
   (A) marrying
   (B) to get married to
   (C) to get married
   (D) to get married with ( )

4. People usually put their money in a ____.
   (A) show
   (B) stamp
   (C) purse
   (D) wine ( )

5. My teacher is singing an English ________, "Yesterday Once More," in class. Everyone is cheering for her.
   (A) song
   (B) sentence
   (C) speaker
   (D) station ( )

6. People in Taipei have to ________ the garbage on time every day. If they miss the garbage collection truck, they have to wait until the next day.
   (A) take away
   (B) take off
   (C) take care of
   (D) take out ( )

7. The happiest time for my dad is when he watches the ________ on TV every night.
   (A) news
   (B) kite
   (C) cook
   (D) subject ( )

8. Besides reviewing the lessons after class, you can also learn more and better by asking ________.
   (A) answers
   (B) questions
   (C) vegetables
   (D) bookstores ( )

9. If you can be more ________ in your learning, you will be a very good learner.
   (A) forgetful
   (B) difficult
   (C) different
   (D) active ( )

10. The girl ________ long hair ________ blue jeans is my classmate.
   (A) has ; and
   (B) with ; with
   (C) with ; in
   (D) in ; with ( )

TEST · 16

※下列各題，請依文意選出一個最適當的答案。

1. I __________ going there by train.
   (A) suggest
   (B) cross
   (C) lose
   (D) add　(　　)

2. Children put on their raincoats __________ it rains outside.
   (A) before
   (B) after
   (C) then
   (D) when　(　　)

3 I was made __________ for hours.
   (A) wait
   (B) waiting
   (C) waited
   (D) to wait　(　　)

4. In Taipei, __________ a lot of rain in spring.
   (A) there are
   (B) we have
   (C) it rains
   (D) it has　(　　)

5. Sir, are you __________ to order now?
   (A) ready
   (B) far
   (C) kind
   (D) busy　(　　)

6. We have a class party today; all the food on the table is __________.
   (A) free
   (B) light
   (C) weekly
   (D) fast ( )

7. I hate spending time with people who keep _________ all the time.
   (A) talking
   (B) to talk
   (C) talked
   (D) taking ( )

8. Some of my friends __________ you spoke yesterday are very kind and friendly.
   (A) that
   (B) to that
   (C) to whom
   (D) who ( )

9. I'll show you around the museum. Please __________ me this way.
   (A) find
   (B) follow
   (C) feel
   (D) forget ( )

10. Coach Lin said that if you don't practice playing basketball more, you cannot __________ the team.
   (A) use
   (B) want
   (C) join
   (D) avoid ( )

TEST · 17

※下列各題，請依文意選出一個最適當的答案。

1. John and Bill would like two _________ of hot coffee.
   (A) glasses
   (B) cups
   (C) bowls
   (D) bottles ( )

2. Mother enjoys _________ some music after work.
   (A) to listen
   (B) to listen to
   (C) listening to
   (D) listening ( )

3. It's _________ for me to do the homework.
   (A) fast
   (B) friendly
   (C) weak
   (D) easy ( )

4. Get up early _________.
   (A) and you'll miss the bus
   (B) if you want to get there early
   (C) so you'll be late for school
   (D) or you'll take the wrong bus ( )

5. I heard her _________ a song to put her baby to sleep.
   (A) sang
   (B) to sing
   (C) sung
   (D) singing ( )

6. I think that to find ________ to questions is an important part of learning.
   (A) answers
   (B) apples
   (C) addresses
   (D) accidents ( )

7. Mr. Chen was having more and more trouble ________ his children.
   (A) understand
   (B) to understand
   (C) understanding
   (D) to understanding ( )

8. I don't understand why many children don't like ________ such as carrots.
   (A) meat
   (B) milk
   (C) vegetables
   (D) coffee ( )

9. Children shouldn't swim in the river because it might not be ________.
   (A) dangerous
   (B) safe
   (C) careful
   (D) expensive ( )

10. 選出正確的一組答案。
   (A) I took his pen without ask him at first.
   (B) I took his pen not first to ask him.
   (C) I took his pen without asking him first.
   (D) I didn't take his pen to ask him first. ( )

TEST · 18

※ 下列各題，請依文意選出一個最適當的答案。

1. The weather is ________ than it was yesterday. I'd really like to go swimming right now.
   (A) hotter
   (B) thinner
   (C) fatter
   (D) bigger　　　　　　　　　　　　　　　　　　　　(　　)

2. "________ do you take a shower?"　"Every day."
   (A) When
   (B) How long
   (C) How often
   (D) What day　　　　　　　　　　　　　　　　　　　(　　)

3. Peter found that Bob ________.
   (A) looked not very happy
   (B) didn't look very happy
   (C) looked not very happily
   (D) didn't look very happily　　　　　　　　　　　　(　　)

4. I have to go home before it gets ________.
   (A) dark
   (B) messy
   (C) close
   (D) real　　　　　　　　　　　　　　　　　　　　　(　　)

5 Do you know ________?
   (A) where does the road go
   (B) when he will come back
   (C) how to do
   (D) why to study English　　　　　　　　　　　　　(　　)

6. I don't believe my cousin is getting __________. He was so short last year when I saw him.
   (A) longer
   (B) prettier
   (C) faster
   (D) taller ( )

7. If one of your hands is full, you can use __________ to open the door.
   (A) other
   (B) the other
   (C) others
   (D) another ( )

8. The math teacher was so angry because some of the students did not __________ the mid-term exam.
   (A) wait for
   (B) do well on
   (C) forget about
   (D) listen to ( )

9. It's no use __________ something sweet to please your boss.
   (A) say
   (B) saying
   (C) to saying
   (D) said ( )

10. People can __________ different cultures if they have the chance to go to other countries.
   (A) experience
   (B) preview
   (C) become
   (D) concentrate ( )

TEST · 19

※下列各題，請依文意選出一個最適當的答案。

1. 選出正確的一組答案。
   (A) Here are his keys.
   (B) Here comes him.
   (C) Here she goes.
   (D) Here are you. ( )

2. I want to be a scientist when I ________ up.
   (A) grow
   (B) get
   (C) go
   (D) give ( )

3. Tibet is called "the ________ of the world."
   (A) house
   (B) town
   (C) roof
   (D) sky ( )

   Tibet 西藏

4. Your sweater is dirty. Why don't you ________?
   (A) take off it
   (B) take it off
   (C) take off
   (D) take sweater off ( )

5. The typhoon is ________. We can go out to play.
   (A) over
   (B) finish
   (C) already
   (D) far ( )

6. A : Ten people were killed in that car accident.
   B : Oh, that's __________.
   (A) great
   (B) interesting
   (C) terrible
   (D) expensive ( )

7. A : How can I get to the train __________?
   B : You can take bus number 5.
   (A) stop
   (B) station
   (C) student
   (D) store ( )

8. Tickets to important games __________.
   (A) do not buy easily
   (B) are not easy bought
   (C) are not easily bought
   (D) never easily buy ( )

9. A __________ officer is running after a young man on the street.
   (A) parents
   (B) police
   (C) prescription
   (D) popular ( )

10. That's __________! She is dressed like a Christmas tree today.
   (A) fake
   (B) famous
   (C) fast
   (D) funny ( )

TEST · 20

※下列各題，請依文意選出一個最適當的答案。

1. Correct eating habits ________ very good for our health.
   (A) is
   (B) are
   (C) do
   (D) has ( )

2. The poor dog is too ________ to stand. It must be sick.
   (A) strong
   (B) weak
   (C) thirsty
   (D) little ( )

3. You ________ early, because the concert on TV was great.
   (A) should come
   (B) shouldn't come
   (C) should have come
   (D) must come ( )

4. You ________ up my life and make me happy.
   (A) turn
   (B) light
   (C) hit
   (D) laugh ( )

5. At ________, Jenny liked David, but now she doesn't.
   (A) all
   (B) better
   (C) most
   (D) first ( )

6. A sudden noise scared the little boy and he started to __________.

(A) come
(B) camp
(C) cry
(D) clean ( )

7. For example, our teacher always tells us __________ trash on the floor.

(A) not throwing
(B) do not throw
(C) not throw
(D) not to throw ( )

8. You can play computer games as long as you __________ doing your homework.

(A) feel
(B) finish
(C) forget
(D) follow ( )

9. My brother has poor eyesight __________ he watches TV very often.

(A) so
(B) be
(C) because
(D) after ( )

10. After the movie, Tom decided to do his homework, and I did __________.

(A) his
(B) hers
(C) mine
(D) yours ( )

TEST · 21

※下列各題，請依文意選出一個最適當的答案。

1. My mp3 player is broken. Do you know ________?
   (A) where I can have it fixed
   (B) how can I have it fixed
   (C) where can I fix it
   (D) how I can have it fix ( )

2. Jordan is a ________ basketball player; even a child knows him.
   (A) famous
   (B) high
   (C) clear
   (D) comfortable ( )

3. I think that ________.
   (A) Tom is best in the class
   (B) Mary is beautifuler than Helen
   (C) English is more hard than Chinese
   (D) this question is easier than that one ( )

4. He ________ this morning.
   (A) ate some medicine
   (B) took any medicines
   (C) had some medicines
   (D) took a little medicine ( )

5. I know the boy, but I can't ________ his name.
   (A) forget
   (B) call
   (C) think
   (D) remember ( )

6. Tom speaks very _________ English and does well on all the tests.
   (A) good
   (B) well
   (C) easy
   (D) old ( )

7. It's kind _________ you to show me the way to the post office.
   (A) for
   (B) to
   (C) with
   (D) of ( )

8. Cathy threw up last night. She must have had some _________ problems.
   (A) barber
   (B) sausage
   (C) stomach
   (D) ambulance ( )

9. There is a shoe _________ near my house. Dad works there.
   (A) maker
   (B) brand
   (C) school
   (D) factory ( )

10. The tests are coming. Students have to _________ for them this week.
    (A) cut
    (B) prepare
    (C) order
    (D) fill ( )

TEST · 22

※下列各題，請依文意選出一個最適當的答案。

1. Sophia needs a house, and her mother is going to buy ________.
   (A) her for it
   (B) one her
   (C) for her
   (D) her one ( )

2. After the typhoon, the ________ of vegetables was high.
   (A) money
   (B) price
   (C) amount
   (D) quality ( )

3. It is too noisy. Tell the children ________.
   (A) don't play so loudly
   (B) stop playing
   (C) not to play so loudly
   (D) to stop to play so loudly ( )

4. He looks like a police officer, but he is really a ________.
   (A) calendar
   (B) reflector
   (C) learner
   (D) writer ( )

5. Making a good decision is never easy, ________ it?
   (A) is
   (B) isn't
   (C) does
   (D) doesn't ( )

6. 選出正確的一組答案。
   (A) On one beautiful morning, he came to see me.
   (B) Do you mind sitting near you?
   (C) I think that he will not come to the party.
   (D) His foot hurt last night. ( )

7. Without a doctor's ________, we can't buy medicine in Taiwan.
   (A) voice
   (B) idea
   (C) prescription
   (D) smile ( )

8. Mr. Li is a very ________ person (VIP) in the school. All the students respect him.
   (A) important
   (B) illegal
   (C) ideal
   (D) identify ( )

   respect 尊敬

9. Here are ten questions. The first three are very easy but ________ are quite hard.
   (A) the other
   (B) others
   (C) the others
   (D) another ( )

10. Mr. Wang is a good ________ in his wife's eyes so she calls him "Mr. Right."
   (A) worker
   (B) businessman
   (C) teacher
   (D) husband ( )

TEST · 23

※下列各題，請依文意選出一個最適當的答案。

1. Tom is seven years old. He is old enough to go to a(n) __________.
   (A) junior high school
   (B) senior high school
   (C) elementary school
   (D) cram school ( )

2. You look tired. Why not __________ home early?
   (A) going
   (B) go
   (C) did you go
   (D) to go ( )

3. All you have to do __________ study hard.
   (A) is
   (B) are
   (C) has
   (D) have ( )

4. Do you mind __________?
   (A) when he leave
   (B) if I turn the radio on
   (C) what does he say
   (D) I opening the window ( )

5. He enjoys __________ basketball very much.
   (A) play the
   (B) play
   (C) playing the
   (D) playing ( )

6. When he came back late, his wife looked __________ at him.
   (A) coldly
   (B) happily
   (C) suddenly
   (D) badly ( )

7. "Wow, your glasses look nice on you. They are so __________," said Mary.
   (A) terrible
   (B) fashionable
   (C) safe
   (D) important ( )

8. I don't like this __________ of coffee. Can you give me Maxwell coffee?
   (A) trade
   (B) mark
   (C) brand
   (D) bill ( )

9. When you go out, don't forget __________ the gas.
   (A) turn off
   (B) to turn off
   (C) turning off
   (D) turn it off ( )

10. In winter, the weather is very cold and the wind will __________ us.
   (A) decorate
   (B) chill
   (C) afraid
   (D) listen ( )

TEST · 24

※下列各題，請依文意選出一個最適當的答案。

1. There was a little boy crying on the street, but no one ________ him.
   (A) frightened
   (B) noticed
   (C) liked
   (D) listened ( )

2. After Dr. Wu ________ my eyes, he said I was OK.
   (A) looked
   (B) glanced
   (C) examined
   (D) watched ( )

3. Before ________ to eat, remember to wash your hands.
   (A) ordering
   (B) finishing
   (C) beginning
   (D) ending ( )

4. I always go to school ________.
   (A) with her
   (B) by a bicycle
   (C) very quick
   (D) in the garden ( )

5. He is ________ to go to senior high school.
   (A) so old
   (B) enough old
   (C) old enough
   (D) such an old boy ( )

6. Mrs. White was sick, so her husband took her to the __________.
   (A) hospital
   (B) restaurant
   (C) police station
   (D) bus stop ( )

7. He shows me his love __________ cooking spaghetti for me.
   (A) about
   (B) in
   (C) with
   (D) by ( )

8. Mom can't see clearly, so she needs a __________ of glasses.
   (A) piece
   (B) cup
   (C) group
   (D) pair ( )

9. A driver should wear a __________, even for a short trip, in Taiwan.
   (A) swimsuit
   (B) life jacket
   (C) sweater
   (D) seatbelt ( )

10. The girl __________ in the pool is my sister.
   (A) swimming
   (B) swims
   (C) is swimming
   (D) swam ( )

TEST · 25

※下列各題，請依文意選出一個最適當的答案。

1. Mary has been to America several times, ________?
   (A) isn't she
   (B) doesn't she
   (C) has she
   (D) hasn't she ( )

2. It's ________ to sell fake rice wine.
   (A) great
   (B) embarrassing
   (C) illegal
   (D) interesting ( )

3. She ________ knows the news. No need to tell her.
   (A) even
   (B) yet
   (C) not
   (D) already ( )

4. John is a good friend of ________.
   (A) me
   (B) my sister's
   (C) her
   (D) your ( )

5. I can't see her, but I can hear her ________.
   (A) voice
   (B) sound
   (C) noise
   (D) tape ( )

6. In order to make our class better, many things still need __________.
   (A) to do
   (B) to be done
   (C) being done
   (D) is doing ( )

7. When Sara has free time, she always reads the magazines __________.
   (A) which she is interested
   (B) which she is interesting to
   (C) she is interesting in
   (D) which interest her ( )

8. Judging by the look of the __________, the weather won't clear up soon.
   (A) sky
   (B) light
   (C) wind
   (D) color ( )

9. According to the NHIP, if you make too many visits to the doctor, you must pay an extra __________.
   (A) watch
   (B) look
   (C) fee
   (D) examination ( )

   > 📖 NHIP 全民健保方案

10. __________ are the windows of our minds.
   (A) Eyes
   (B) Hands
   (C) Glasses
   (D) Televisions ( )

TEST · 26

※下列各題，請依文意選出一個最適當的答案。

1. To play computer games ________.
   (A) are a lot of fun because they are exciting
   (B) has a lot of fun
   (C) which are exciting is a lot of fun
   (D) will be confused with us ( )

2. I don't like those watches. They are just like ________.
   (A) ideas
   (B) toys
   (C) brands
   (D) goods ( )

3. Betty has ________ time. She can't go to a baseball game.
   (A) a little
   (B) little
   (C) few
   (D) a few ( )

4. Elephants are the ________ animals on land.
   (A) most expensive
   (B) smallest
   (C) oldest
   (D) largest ( )

5. I live in a three-room ________.
   (A) apartment
   (B) wardrobe
   (C) calculator
   (D) break ( )

6. Avoid __________ embarrassing questions when you are having a conversation.
   (A) to ask
   (B) asking
   (C) to speak
   (D) speaking ( )

7. When the big __________ and the heavy rain came, we stayed at home.
   (A) weather
   (B) news
   (C) shower
   (D) typhoon ( )

8. Mary doesn't __________ Mother's Day, because her mother died last year.
   (A) prepare
   (B) notice
   (C) celebrate
   (D) thank ( )

9. Not only you but also she __________ a hardworking student.
   (A) are
   (B) is
   (C) to be
   (D) were ( )

10. Amy has to do most of the __________ when her parents are not at home.
   (A) homework
   (B) housework
   (C) firework
   (D) study ( )

TEST · 27

※ 下列各題，請依文意選出一個最適當的答案。

1. Eve is very sad today, and __________ you can help her.
   (A) how
   (B) when
   (C) why
   (D) maybe ( )

2. My computer doesn't __________, so I can't do anything.
   (A) play
   (B) move
   (C) work
   (D) show ( )

3. If there __________ no air, people couldn't live.
   (A) is
   (B) has
   (C) were
   (D) was ( )

4. Mary was sick. The doctor gave her a __________ in the arm.
   (A) bite
   (B) hurt
   (C) shot
   (D) shut ( )

5. He is less __________ than she.
   (A) taller
   (B) the taller
   (C) the tallest
   (D) tall ( )

6. When there was an earthquake, I __________ the house moving.
   (A) rode
   (B) felt
   (C) fell
   (D) weeded ( )

7. Tomorrow we will have an English test. I have already reviewed the book __________ times.
   (A) one
   (B) twice
   (C) once
   (D) several ( )

8. They couldn't find John in Taipei. __________, he has gone to America.
   (A) Finally
   (B) In fact
   (C) Suddenly
   (D) By the way ( )

9. You would like to know if I will go to the movies tonight, __________?
   (A) did you
   (B) will I
   (C) wouldn't you
   (D) won't I ( )

10. If someone breaks the rule, the teacher may ask him __________.
   (A) why did he make the mistake
   (B) why he did it
   (C) why they happened
   (D) why did he do it ( )

TEST · 28

※ 下列各題，請依文意選出一個最適當的答案。

1. ________ are famous.
   (A) Susan and Tony's schools
   (B) Susan and Tony's school
   (C) Susan's and Tony's schools
   (D) Susan's and Tony's school ( )

2. On the wall ________ two pictures.
   (A) is
   (B) has
   (C) are
   (D) have ( )

3. Miss Martin ________ her bookstore at seven every morning.
   (A) open
   (B) opens
   (C) opening
   (D) to open ( )

4. Karen eats a lot, so she is getting ________.
   (A) more fat
   (B) the fattest
   (C) much fattest
   (D) fatter and fatter ( )

5. It is said that ________ comes from Italy.
   (A) pizza
   (B) tea
   (C) coke
   (D) steak ( )

6. Yesterday Mary and I played cards. She __________ one hundred dollars from me.
   (A) gave
   (B) sent
   (C) won
   (D) wore ( )

7. __________ we don't have enough money, we can't buy the house with a swimming pool.
   (A) Since
   (B) After
   (C) But
   (D) Though ( )

8. Though Kevin doesn't do well on math tests, he never __________ studying for them.
   (A) uses up
   (B) gives up
   (C) makes up
   (D) look up ( )

9. At the __________ of summer vacation, students always feel sad because they have to go back to school soon.
   (A) start
   (B) plan
   (C) coming
   (D) end ( )

10. Please send my best __________ to your family. If I have time, I will go to visit them.
   (A) wishes
   (B) taxis
   (C) bicycles
   (D) buses ( )

TEST · 29

※ 下列各題，請依文意選出一個最適當的答案。

1. "Isn't she a nurse?" "__________ a student."
   (A) No, she isn't
   (B) Yes, she is
   (C) No, she is
   (D) Yes, both are ( )

2. Sue is good at gardening. She has green __________.
   (A) feet
   (B) heads
   (C) fingers
   (D) faces ( )

3. Don't make me __________! I'm serious about it.
   (A) laugh
   (B) to laugh
   (C) laughing
   (D) laughed ( )

4. She never gets up late, but her brother __________.
   (A) always does
   (B) is always
   (C) does always
   (D) doesn't, either ( )

5. As for children, ice cream is their __________ food in summer.
   (A) different
   (B) favorite
   (C) talented
   (D) strict ( )

6. One of _________ in Mr. Chang's Chinese class comes from New York.
   (A) student
   (B) the student
   (C) students
   (D) the students ( )

7. The most _________ weather in Taiwan is in September, October and November. It is cool in those months.
   (A) greedy
   (B) comfortable
   (C) snowy
   (D) sudden ( )

8. People say that A-mei lives on the sixth _________ of this beautiful building.
   (A) door
   (B) window
   (C) towel
   (D) floor ( )

9. There are famous universities in _________, like Oxford and Cambridge.
   (A) Japan
   (B) England
   (C) America
   (D) Canada ( )

10. 選出正確的一組答案。
   (A) Whose are these boxs?
   (B) Whose guiter is this?
   (C) He walked up to the table and put a cup on it.
   (D) Here is your jacket. Put on it. ( )

TEST · 30

※下列各題，請依文意選出一個最適當的答案。

1. When the sky is blue and ________, we know that it will be a sunny day.
   (A) dark
   (B) dirty
   (C) clear
   (D) rainy　　(　)

2. His idea is different from ________.
   (A) I
   (B) mine
   (C) my
   (D) me　　(　)

3. "What day is today?"　"It is ________."
   (A) May 2
   (B) Sunday
   (C) fine
   (D) spring　　(　)

4. France is the biggest country in ________.
   (A) America
   (B) Asia
   (C) Africa
   (D) Europe　　(　)

5. He has stayed away from school ________ last month.
   (A) from
   (B) since
   (C) for
   (D) before　　(　)

6. All he could do was say good-bye to Rose, __________ his hand.

   (A) wave
   (B) waves
   (C) waved
   (D) waving ( )

7. When his mother is not at home, Johnny always __________ to cook dinner for his family.

   (A) volunteers
   (B) vacuums
   (C) cleans
   (D) mops ( )

8. The price of the 28-__________ TV is so low that I can't wait to buy it.

   (A) inchs
   (B) inches
   (C) inch
   (D) inched ( )

9. We should recycle in order not to produce too much __________.

   (A) money
   (B) tower
   (C) garbage
   (D) clothes ( )

10. July 4 is the Independence Day of the United States. __________, they will have a big celebration on that day.

   (A) Of course
   (B) Worst of all
   (C) So far
   (D) No way ( )

TEST · 31

※ 下列各題，請依文意選出一個最適當的答案。

1. John passed all the tests, __________ made his parents very proud of him.
   (A) that
   (B) who
   (C) which
   (D) whom ( )

2. We need a lot of rain and warm, __________ weather.
   (A) humid
   (B) greasy
   (C) delicious
   (D) sudden ( )

3. How many __________?
   (A) days is there in a year
   (B) seasons are there of a year
   (C) people does in your family have
   (D) lessons are there in the book ( )

4. I rang the doorbell, but it didn't work. It must be __________.
   (A) living
   (B) confused
   (C) worried
   (D) dead ( )

5. They had a good time, __________.
   (A) and so had we
   (B) and so did we
   (C) and neither had we
   (D) we did, too ( )

6. The rooms were dirty after Mother went to Japan, so John decided to __________ them by himself.
   (A) weed
   (B) keep
   (C) throw
   (D) clean ( )

7. I like playing __________, so my brother bought me __________ as my birthday present.
   (A) baseball , baseball
   (B) a baseball , baseball
   (C) baseball , a baseball
   (D) the baseball , a baseball ( )

8. Traveling is my favorite pastime. I hope that I will go to all the __________ in the world.
   (A) countries
   (B) food
   (C) seasons
   (D) vacations ( )

9. __________ are very popular in Taipei now. Almost every young man has one.
   (A) Subways
   (B) Cell phones
   (C) Bakeries
   (D) Museums ( )

10. I am now in the third year of junior high. I feel that time __________ on fast.
   (A) stops
   (B) saves
   (C) moves
   (D) speaks ( )

TEST · 32

※下列各題，請依文意選出一個最適當的答案。

1. There __________ several important holidays in October.
   (A) is
   (B) are
   (C) have
   (D) has ( )

2. When you go traveling, smiles are a very useful world __________.
   (A) language
   (B) pollution
   (C) food
   (D) program ( )

3. The streets in New York __________.
   (A) are busier than those in Taipei
   (B) is busier than any city in Taiwan
   (C) is more busier than any other city in Taiwan
   (D) are more busy than those in Taiwan ( )

4. I drank several __________ a day.
   (A) glass of water
   (B) glasses of water
   (C) glass water
   (D) water glasses ( )

5. If you catch a cold, it's better to __________ medicine.
   (A) drink
   (B) take
   (C) eat
   (D) make ( )

6. The master and his dog _________ had gone hunting together last Saturday were never seen again.
   (A) that
   (B) which
   (C) of which
   (D) who ( )

7. Life today is quite _________ from life one hundred years ago.
   (A) same
   (B) quiet
   (C) different
   (D) slow ( )

8. Jack is smart and studies hard. _________ he will be the Chinese Einstein.
   (A) May be
   (B) Perhaps
   (C) Never
   (D) Already ( )

9. After traveling in Europe for one year, Jack has undergone a great _________.
   (A) sweater
   (B) weather
   (C) change
   (D) cram ( )

10. I could hear my _________ beating when I met my first lover by chance.
   (A) bread
   (B) wedding
   (C) virus
   (D) heart ( )

TEST・33

※下列各題，請依文意選出一個最適當的答案。

1. Though he has studied the lesson three times, it is still ________ to him.
   (A) active
   (B) ideal
   (C) fashionable
   (D) strange ( )

2. Hopes ________ a colorful life.
   (A) create
   (B) avoid
   (C) envy
   (D) end ( )

3. I saw a boy ________ I think was your student.
   (A) who
   (B) whom
   (C) whose
   (D) which ( )

4. I ________ how to play the piano since ________.
   (A) have been learning ; I was six
   (B) learned ; last year
   (C) had learned ; two years ago
   (D) have learned ; two year ( )

5. He made several ________ through stocks.
   (A) middle
   (B) candy
   (C) oil
   (D) million ( )

6. The use of ________ makes people write letters more often.
   (A) e-mail
   (B) plane
   (C) phone
   (D) radio ( )

7. Every day there is exciting and surprising news all over the ________.
   (A) mouth
   (B) world
   (C) trouble
   (D) envelope ( )

8. ________ a lot of rain in New York yesterday.
   (A) Where there was
   (B) It fell
   (C) There had
   (D) We had ( )

9. Michael Jordan is a good ________ for many basketball players.
   (A) animal
   (B) question
   (C) example
   (D) nation ( )

10. ________ people went to Kenting to watch the shooting stars.
   (A) Thousands
   (B) Thousand of
   (C) Thousands of
   (D) Two thousands of ( )

TEST · 34

※下列各題，請依文意選出一個最適當的答案。

1. Concentrate on your studies, ________?
   (A) will they
   (B) will you
   (C) don't you
   (D) won't you ( )

2. It is dangerous for motorcyclists to ________ traffic rules.
   (A) follow
   (B) break
   (C) meet
   (D) take ( )

3. He has no house ________.
   (A) to live
   (B) to live in
   (C) which he can live
   (D) where is good to live ( )

4. The boys ________ their house tomorrow evening.
   (A) left
   (B) leave
   (C) has left
   (D) leaving ( )

5. Japanese and Korean singers are now ________ with young people in Taiwan.
   (A) difficult
   (B) possible
   (C) popular
   (D) dirty ( )

6. Most stores have _________ on the wall to watch people buying things there.
   (A) cameras
   (B) radios
   (C) tapes
   (D) cell phones ( )

7. Students are very busy in Taiwan because there are too many _________ for them to learn.
   (A) semesters
   (B) subjects
   (C) housework
   (D) buildings ( )

8. People learn well and quickly when they feel that things are _________ to them.
   (A) interesting
   (B) boring
   (C) confusing
   (D) worrying ( )

9. Bob is the tallest in my class, and I'm sure he is taller than _________ student in your class.
   (A) any
   (B) any other
   (C) all the other
   (D) other ( )

10. When _________ come, you need to catch them. Or they will pass fast.
   (A) noises
   (B) pollutions
   (C) opportunities
   (D) allowances ( )

TEST · 35

※下列各題，請依文意選出一個最適當的答案。

1. He drove his truck ________ fruit to the market.
   (A) full
   (B) was full of
   (C) which full of
   (D) full of ( )

2. In such cold weather I ________ my winter coat all day.
   (A) put on
   (B) wear
   (C) am putting on
   (D) take off ( )

3. Mary and John can hardly ________ meeting each other because they work in the same office.
   (A) produce
   (B) make
   (C) keep
   (D) avoid ( )

4. The more you exercise, the ________ you are.
   (A) stronger
   (B) harder
   (C) quieter
   (D) unhappier ( )

5. My sports shoes are too small; they ________ my feet.
   (A) enjoy
   (B) want
   (C) hurt
   (D) jump ( )

6. It's not right to ________ someone behind his or her back.
   (A) welcome
   (B) criticize
   (C) waste
   (D) fix ( )

7. Don't waste your money ________ useless things, such as cute dolls and posters of movie stars.
   (A) in
   (B) to buy
   (C) buying
   (D) for ( )

8. The room was dark and I ________ my head against the desk.
   (A) spent
   (B) shut
   (C) bumped
   (D) quitted ( )

9. If everyone follows traffic rules, ________ will be fewer and fewer.
   (A) accidents
   (B) people
   (C) cans
   (D) taxis ( )

10. Dictionaries are very ________ for people learning languages.
    (A) tall
    (B) embarrassed
    (C) polite
    (D) useful ( )

TEST · 36

※ 下列各題，請依文意選出一個最適當的答案。

1. It is illegal for people under 18 years old to ride ________.
   (A) bicycles
   (B) motorcycles
   (C) horses
   (D) buses ( )

2. They ________ her about her freckles.
   (A) teased
   (B) drowned
   (C) rented
   (D) pretended ( )

3. Although John is not good in main subjects, he surely has ________ for sports.
   (A) seat
   (B) size
   (C) life
   (D) talent ( )

main 主要

4. He ________ three hours studying English last night.
   (A) cost
   (B) took
   (C) spent
   (D) needed ( )

5. ________ are of the same age.
   (A) You, she and I
   (B) I, you and she
   (C) You, I and she
   (D) She, I and you ( )

6. The __________ was attracted by her beautiful voice.
   (A) contest
   (B) stage
   (C) audience
   (D) protest ( )

7. The population of Taipei City is larger than __________ of Kaohsiung.
   (A) ×
   (B) those
   (C) this
   (D) that ( )

8. I would like to meet you tonight if __________ convenient for you.
   (A) you are
   (B) it's
   (C) it will be
   (D) I'm ( )

9. Life in __________ countries is new and interesting for travelers.
   (A) violent
   (B) young
   (C) foreign
   (D) boring ( )

10. I bought the bicycle two years ago but it still looks like __________.
   (A) a new one
   (B) new
   (C) that is new
   (D) a his new bicycle ( )

TEST · 37

※下列各題，請依文意選出一個最適當的答案。

1. I ________ live in the U. S., but now I live in Taiwan.
   (A) used
   (B) am used to
   (C) was used to
   (D) used to ( )

2. He quit ________ in the city and moved to the country.
   (A) work
   (B) to work
   (C) working
   (D) worked ( )

3. Susan is not popular in her class because she ________ too much.
   (A) shows up
   (B) shows off
   (C) shuts up
   (D) stays up ( )

4. The package has been ________ to Uncle Bob's house.
   (A) built
   (B) told
   (C) sent
   (D) drawn ( )

5. How about ________ a cup of tea right now?
   (A) have
   (B) to having
   (C) having
   (D) to have ( )

6. 選出正確的一組答案。
   (A) My brother came home on the morning of May 1, 2000.
   (B) He sang the song good enough.
   (C) He is the only one child in his family.
   (D) I know who is that man. ( )

7. I need a car, but I don't have enough money to buy __________.
   (A) it
   (B) car
   (C) one
   (D) this ( )

8. Most people like Thai food a lot because it __________ sour and spicy.
   (A) sounds
   (B) smells
   (C) tastes
   (D) seems ( )

9. People should be __________ while they are studying in the library.
   (A) quiet
   (B) quite
   (C) public
   (D) possible ( )

10. Jackie failed the tests many times, but he never gave up. __________, he passed all the tests.
    (A) Finally
    (B) Immediately
    (C) Particularly
    (D) Truly ( )

TEST · 38

※ 下列各題，請依文意選出一個最適當的答案。

1. Mark takes the ________ to school every morning.
   (A) traffic
   (B) bookworm
   (C) PE
   (D) MRT ( )

2. It's hot in here. Please turn the ________ on.
   (A) communication
   (B) software
   (C) air-conditioner
   (D) conversation ( )

3. I would like you ________.
   (A) coming right away
   (B) to practice every day
   (C) buy the morning paper
   (D) do it on your own ( )

4. All you have to do is take good ________ of yourself.
   (A) mate
   (B) machine
   (C) care
   (D) grade ( )

5. "________" "I'm a dancer."
   (A) Who are you?
   (B) What do you?
   (C) What are you?
   (D) How are you? ( )

6. Aunt Annie has two sons who ________ from NTU.

   (A) graduated
   (B) smiled
   (C) traveled
   (D) criticized ( )

📖 NTU 台灣大學

7. Mom won't ________ Wendy marry a man who is lazy and dirty.

   (A) let
   (B) tell
   (C) decide
   (D) want ( )

8. Princess Diana, who was ________ to Prince Charles, is dead.

   (A) seen
   (B) hoped
   (C) married
   (D) packed ( )

9. He works very hard. It's not ________ that he's always ________.

   (A) surprised ; tired
   (B) surprising ; tiring
   (C) surprising ; tired
   (D) surprised ; tiring ( )

10. In a fast-food restaurant, Jean ordered not only fried chicken ________.

   (A) but pizza
   (B) also a hamburger
   (C) or a milk shake
   (D) and an order of French fries ( )

TEST · 39

※ 下列各題，請依文意選出一個最適當的答案。

1. All good things come to ________.
   (A) he who waits
   (B) him to wait
   (C) which is waiting
   (D) waiting man　　(　　)

2. No matter how hard he tries, he still can't ________ it.
   (A) bump
   (B) know
   (C) make
   (D) graduate　　(　　)

3. ________, you will get better grades.
   (A) Study some every evening
   (B) If you study that hard
   (C) Don't listen to your teacher
   (D) Try to study harder　　(　　)

4. Some people think that to be nice to everyone is a(n) ________ goal.
   (A) invisible
   (B) impossible
   (C) impolite
   (D) impressed　　(　　)

5. We've already gone on 20 miles ________.
   (A) father
   (B) farther
   (C) funnier
   (D) farmer　　(　　)

6. My parents told my brother ________ because it's a bad habit.
   (A) to not smoke
   (B) not to smoke
   (C) don't smoke
   (D) not smoking ( )

7. The teacher asked Eddie not to ________ other students' homework.
   (A) care
   (B) copy
   (C) solve
   (D) kill ( )

8. I enjoy ________ to the library, ________ I can read books and magazines.
   (A) going ; which
   (B) to go ; where
   (C) to go ; that
   (D) going ; where ( )

9. Mayday is very popular all over Taiwan. All the fans cheer and ________ at their concerts.
   (A) applaud
   (B) imagine
   (C) produce
   (D) punch ( )

10. In the early 1800s, poor children in America were made to work ________.
    (A) up and down
    (B) day and night
    (C) to and fro
    (D) back and forth ( )

TEST · 40

※下列各題，請依文意選出一個最適當的答案。

1. These are the jeans which ________ NT 2,500 in the department store.
   (A) take
   (B) spend
   (C) cost
   (D) buy ( )

2. I want him not to ________ like a girl.
   (A) manage
   (B) act
   (C) link
   (D) allow ( )

3. Here is the boy ________ pen has been stolen.
   (A) who
   (B) whom
   (C) whose
   (D) that ( )

4. My uncle drives ________ to be the winner.
   (A) well enough
   (B) good enough
   (C) enough well
   (D) enough good ( )

5. Did you ________ your homework last weekend?
   (A) finish doing
   (B) practice to do
   (C) trying doing
   (D) enjoy to do ( )

6. Peter has trouble in learning to use a computer; therefore, he always feels __________ in class.
   (A) boring
   (B) bore
   (C) bored
   (D) bare ( )

7. Everybody knows that people can't live __________ water and oxygen.
   (A) away
   (B) without
   (C) during
   (D) among ( )

8. The teacher who is good at __________ problems teaches us math.
   (A) solving
   (B) blushing
   (C) drawing
   (D) sending ( )

9. I saw the cat __________ into the washing machine. Poor cat!
   (A) jumped
   (B) which jumped
   (C) who jumping
   (D) have jumped ( )

10. My little sister is two years junior __________. However, she is taller than I.
   (A) than I
   (B) to I
   (C) than me
   (D) to me ( )

TEST · 41

※下列各題，請依文意選出一個最適當的答案。

1. So far as I know, there is still no water in some people's houses ________ the typhoon.
   (A) because of
   (B) a number of
   (C) an amount of
   (D) a kind of ( )

2. I forgot the ________ all of a sudden on the stage.
   (A) lines
   (B) roads
   (C) streets
   (D) maps ( )

3. All you have to do ________ inside and study hard.
   (A) are to sit
   (B) sit
   (C) is sit
   (D) are sitting ( )

4. You had better ________ carefully on the highway.
   (A) build
   (B) park
   (C) drive
   (D) tease ( )

5. "When is your ________ exam?" "Next Wednesday."
   (A) funny
   (B) dead
   (C) troublesome
   (D) final ( )

6. After the typhoon struck Taiwan, the traffic of Taipei turned messy. We could see traffic __________ everywhere.
   (A) jams
   (B) passengers
   (C) points
   (D) dreams ( )

7. It's been a long time since we graduated from school. Luckily, we have __________ all these years.
   (A) came up to
   (B) stayed in touch
   (C) stolen a glance
   (D) worked out ( )

8. As soon as I __________ David tomorrow, I'll invite him to my party.
   (A) will meet
   (B) am going to meet
   (C) meet
   (D) met ( )

9. I was born on May 10th. What __________ were you born on?
   (A) season
   (B) date
   (C) month
   (D) year ( )

10. Mother had me __________ to my uncle in the U.S., and I had the letter __________ this morning.
   (A) write ; mail
   (B) written ; mailed
   (C) write ; mailed
   (D) to write ; to mail ( )

TEST · 42

※下列各題，請依文意選出一個最適當的答案。

1. In the cup ________ some coffee.
   (A) is
   (B) has
   (C) have
   (D) are ( )

2. Reading science fiction requires you to use your ________.
   (A) money
   (B) imagination
   (C) dream
   (D) system ( )

3. The boys sitting over there ________.
   (A) were eating lunch together and talked to each other
   (B) were having a good time playing a computer game
   (C) were felt very good talking to each other
   (D) stand up suddenly and left the classroom ( )

4. One ________ is equal to two point five four centimeters.
   (A) inch
   (B) size
   (C) time
   (D) way ( )

equal to 等於

5. A friend of mine owns a shoe factory. His shoe factory ________ more than 30 thousand pairs of shoes a year.
   (A) tells
   (B) produces
   (C) believes
   (D) travels ( )

6. Our class had a picnic in Youth Park. There we saw __________.
   (A) a lot of tree
   (B) a lot of child
   (C) many bird
   (D) many people ( )

7. A : Which do you like more, the green one or the red one?
   B : I don't know __________. They're both nice.
   (A) which to buy
   (B) which I buy
   (C) that I should buy
   (D) which should I buy ( )

8. I've not been able to __________ clearly lately. I think I have to have my eyes examined.
   (A) see
   (B) confirm
   (C) fix
   (D) exercise ( )

9. I would give some of my money to poor people __________ I were rich.
   (A) because
   (B) so
   (C) if
   (D) when ( )

10. Most teenagers like Show Lo because they think he can tell __________ well.
   (A) jokes
   (B) colors
   (C) heros
   (D) reasons ( )

TEST · 43

※下列各題，請依文意選出一個最適當的答案。

1. Students should follow the school rules. First, students should arrive at school ________.
   (A) in time
   (B) at a time
   (C) on time
   (D) with care ( )

2. Some people believe there are aliens in outer ________.
   (A) star
   (B) space
   (C) school
   (D) jeep ( )

3. Please let me ________ you a coffee.
   (A) buy
   (B) to buy
   (C) buying
   (D) bought ( )

4. Making a good decision may ________.
   (A) cost you your life
   (B) take you a long time
   (C) spend lots of time
   (D) make you feel sorry ( )

5. Both ________ will come to the party.
   (A) you and me
   (B) my parents
   (C) we
   (D) them ( )

6. All the students of our school are so nervous because we are going to have an English __________ with our foreign teacher next Friday.
   (A) communication
   (B) computer
   (C) convenience
   (D) conversation ( )

7. Once I heard the song "That's What Friends Are For". It made me __________ my best friend, who is in Hawaii now.
   (A) think on
   (B) think of
   (C) think up
   (D) thanks to ( )

8. Be sure to wear a __________ when you go out. It's freezing cold outside.
   (A) T-shirt
   (B) pants
   (C) sweater
   (D) shorts ( )

9. There __________ several important games since we met several weeks ago.
   (A) have been
   (B) has had
   (C) were
   (D) will have ( )

10. I want to buy the house __________.
   (A) the Wangs live in it
   (B) that is next to the Wangs'
   (C) which is a big garden
   (D) there are six rooms in it ( )

TEST · 44

※ 下列各題，請依文意選出一個最適當的答案。

1. My older brother is going to ________ to study. He is going to leave us for Kaohsiung tomorrow.
   (A) future
   (B) college
   (C) examination
   (D) underground ( )

2. She went ________.
   (A) to Tom's home at 6:30
   (B) her home in five o'clock
   (C) home on 4:30
   (D) to school at seven-eleven o'clock ( )

3. "Who ________ a bicycle there?" "Joe is."
   (A) rides
   (B) drive
   (C) is riding
   (D) is driving ( )

4. I want to know if you ________ to my party tonight.
   (A) come
   (B) came
   (C) will come
   (D) have come ( )

5. Mr. Brown was so lazy and careless a cook ________.
   (A) as to be fired by his boss
   (B) in order not to please his customers
   (C) enough to scare most of the customers away
   (D) that to offer a terrible meal ( )

6. Mary's family is looking for a new apartment. It has to include all furniture and have two _________ bedrooms, a clean kitchen and two big bathrooms.
   (A) handsome
   (B) air-conditioned
   (C) invisible
   (D) alone ( )

7. I can't find my keys but I remember _________ them on the table.
   (A) putting
   (B) to put
   (C) put
   (D) have put ( )

8. This is the subject in which I can learn about a lot of things that happened in the past. The subject is _________.
   (A) history
   (B) English
   (C) music
   (D) physical education ( )

9. It's not necessary to feel sad about getting a bad grade on the test. _________, no one can get good grades all the time.
   (A) After all
   (B) Each other
   (C) At least
   (D) In case ( )

10. After you wash your hands, dry them with this _________.
    (A) towel
    (B) tower
    (C) town
    (D) toy ( )

TEST · 45

※下列各題，請依文意選出一個最適當的答案。

1. You look worried. What ________?
   (A) happened
   (B) was happened
   (C) did you happen
   (D) happening ( )

2. These are the children who have been very ________ to grownups. Everyone likes them a lot.
   (A) stupid
   (B) possible
   (C) polluted
   (D) polite ( )

3. Mother always prepares us ________.
   (A) big breakfast
   (B) a big breakfast
   (C) have breakfast
   (D) eat breakfast ( )

4. Tell me the truth. Don't beat around the ________.
   (A) push
   (B) woman
   (C) policeman
   (D) bush ( )

5. She is ________ money for her trip to Kenting.
   (A) believing
   (B) saving
   (C) copying
   (D) cooking ( )

6. A : ________ here.
   B : Really, that's a surprise. I thought they'd come.
   (A) Neither John nor Fred is
   (B) Both John and Fred are
   (C) Neither John nor Fred aren't
   (D) Both John and Fred aren't ( )

7. The weather often changes very fast in Taipei, but it is usually ________ every day in Kaohsiung.
   (A) the same as
   (B) the same
   (C) as same as
   (D) same ( )

8. When Bill talks to others in a ________ voice, we know he is going to ask them for help.
   (A) gentle
   (B) gently
   (C) quite
   (D) quietly ( )

9. Tom : I haven't seen the movie "Kingsman" yet.
   Sue : ________
   Tom : Then, let's go to the movie this Sunday.
   (A) So do I
   (B) So have I
   (C) Neither do I
   (D) Neither have I ( )

10. He dropped from the tree and then fell to the ________.
    (A) sky
    (B) guitar
    (C) ground
    (D) subject ( )

TEST · 46

※ 下列各題，請依文意選出一個最適當的答案。

1. The player was so tired that he couldn't but fall ________.
   (A) alone
   (B) alive
   (C) along
   (D) asleep ( )

2. Eric works ________ that he is sure to get good grades.
   (A) hardly
   (B) hardly so
   (C) good enough
   (D) so hard ( )

3. Many English words are ________ from French: beef, pork and mutton, for example.
   (A) borrowed
   (B) rented
   (C) lend
   (D) kept ( )

4. As I walked into the classroom, I heard my name ________.
   (A) call
   (B) called
   (C) calling
   (D) was called ( )

5. Father is too busy, so I will help him ________ his car.
   (A) wash
   (B) to washing
   (C) washing
   (D) for washing ( )

6. Linda hopes she can own a large house with a beautiful _________ in the near future.
   (A) problem
   (B) village
   (C) garden
   (D) accident ( )

7. A : _________, I'm going on the trip to Hualien; I don't like him much anyway.
   B : He _________ a big mouth.
   (A) Whether he to come ; had
   (B) Whether or not he comes ; has
   (C) If or not he comes ; has
   (D) If he will come ; had ( )

8. When he _________ enough money, he's going to travel all over the world.
   (A) will make
   (B) made
   (C) makes
   (D) is made ( )

9. John's mother makes him _________ the lawn every week.
   (A) feed
   (B) weed
   (C) wash
   (D) wish ( )

10. The street vendor _________ an old carpet on his stand, trying to sell it to a foreigner.
   (A) spread
   (B) criticized
   (C) created
   (D) linked ( )

TEST · 47

※下列各題，請依文意選出一個最適當的答案。

1. Last weekend, I got a nice jacket. Mom ________.
   (A) bought it to me
   (B) bought me it
   (C) gave it to me
   (D) gave me it ( )

2. The sun is ________ outside, but it is raining in my mind.
   (A) developing
   (B) entering
   (C) shining
   (D) fighting ( )

3. The children entered the garden through the ________.
   (A) gate
   (B) fake
   (C) fire
   (D) light ( )

4. The doctor is so busy ________ lunch.
   (A) to eat
   (B) enough to eat
   (C) that he eats
   (D) that he can't eat ( )

5. He turned ________ the light and drove darkness away from his place at once.
   (A) off
   (B) on
   (C) over
   (D) down ( )

6. Do you know a shop __________ I can find computer programs?
   (A) which
   (B) that
   (C) where
   (D) of which ( )

7. The __________ of heavy traffic makes modern people get angry easily.
   (A) street
   (B) number
   (C) envelope
   (D) noise ( )

8. It's __________ for such a gentleman like him to say four-letter words.
   (A) usual
   (B) unusual
   (C) certain
   (D) uncertain ( )

9. "__________ the change," he said to the poor girl who sold matches on the street corner.
   (A) Look
   (B) Drink
   (C) Peep
   (D) Keep ( )

10. Every evening, all my family and I get together and eat dinner in the __________.
   (A) garage
   (B) dining room
   (C) bedroom
   (D) restroom ( )

TEST · 48

※下列各題，請依文意選出一個最適當的答案。

1. I asked my son ________ watch TV too much.
   (A) didn't
   (B) to not
   (C) not
   (D) not to ( )

2. ________ the weather like in England last April?
   (A) How's
   (B) What's
   (C) How was
   (D) What was ( )

3. He is an active learner. He learns better ________ asking questions.
   (A) in
   (B) with
   (C) by
   (D) on ( )

4. Bill, go ________ the door.
   (A) sink
   (B) answer
   (C) insist
   (D) respond ( )

5. He ________ the stamp and stuck it on the envelope.
   (A) looked
   (B) cooked
   (C) ruined
   (D) licked ( )

6. With the handsome star walking _________ her, Jane felt nervous and excited.
   (A) toward
   (B) over
   (C) on
   (D) off ( )

7. My grandmother gave me a music _________ as my birthday present.
   (A) box
   (B) fox
   (C) six
   (D) mix ( )

8. After _________ from the U.S., President Ma told the press he would do a lot for Taiwan's economy.
   (A) going
   (B) returning
   (C) bringing
   (D) reaching ( )

9. Every time you enter the park, you can always find some new _________ there.
   (A) faces
   (B) seasons
   (C) tips
   (D) typhoons ( )

10. The ground is _________, so it must have rained last night.
   (A) wet
   (B) dry
   (C) vacuumed
   (D) mopped ( )

TEST · 49

※下列各題，請依文意選出一個最適當的答案。

1. I remembered seeing the man ________.
   (A) which Tom spoke to
   (B) Tom talked to
   (C) who Mark worked with him
   (D) whom Mark worked ( )

2. A: How do you like your eggs?
   B: ________
   (A) Give me a dozen.
   (B) Sunny-side up, please.
   (C) They are very tasty.
   (D) None of your business. ( )

3. Book One is ________ than Book Five.
   (A) very easy
   (B) more easy
   (C) very easier
   (D) much easier ( )

4. I ________ whether I might ask you a question.
   (A) wonder
   (B) wander
   (C) wound
   (D) would ( )

5. Would you like to ________ a message for him?
   (A) think
   (B) boil
   (C) leave
   (D) arrive ( )

6. On average, __________ more than 50 thousand passengers taking the subway to work every day.
   (A) there is
   (B) there have
   (C) there have been
   (D) there will be ( )

7. A tea break is a period of time in which you can relax yourself by having some tea and __________.
   (A) snakes
   (B) shakes
   (C) shots
   (D) snacks ( )

8. If you play the piano too __________ at night, you'll bother your neighbors.
   (A) illegally
   (B) clearly
   (C) loudly
   (D) fashionably ( )

9. If you run __________ a red light, you may be fined NT 1800 dollars.
   (A) through
   (B) though
   (C) thought
   (D) thousand ( )

10. When someone is __________ by a snake, he should find out what kind it is first.
   (A) heard
   (B) found
   (C) slept
   (D) bitten ( )

TEST · 50

※ 下列各題，請依文意選出一個最適當的答案。

1. I can't remember __________ from here.
   (A) where do we go
   (B) where are we going
   (C) where we should go
   (D) how far should we be going ( )

2. Before __________ the house, please take off your shoes.
   (A) entering
   (B) forgetting
   (C) preparing
   (D) noticing ( )

3. They __________ a famous high school near Keelung.
   (A) open
   (B) live
   (C) teach
   (D) attend ( )

4. You __________ last night. You look tired.
   (A) don't sleep at all
   (B) must go to bed late
   (C) must not sleep
   (D) must have studied late ( )

5. Some of the students have trouble __________ what to buy.
   (A) choose
   (B) chose
   (C) choosing
   (D) chooses ( )

6. My brother is heavier than I, but he can __________ higher than I.
   (A) volunteer
   (B) spell
   (C) jump
   (D) invite ( )

7. Most young girls __________ tall and cool boys, though those boys are not always ideal mates.
   (A) are proud of
   (B) are fond of
   (C) are afraid of
   (D) are tired of ( )

8. I make __________ look like a football player.
   (A) me
   (B) myself
   (C) me to
   (D) myself to ( )

9. My bedroom is on the second floor. I felt hungry last night, so I went __________ to the kitchen on the first floor to find something to eat.
   (A) downstair
   (B) downstairs
   (C) upstair
   (D) upstairs ( )

10. A language will no longer live and grow __________.
   (A) when people stop to speak it
   (B) people stop speaking
   (C) when people stop speaking it
   (D) to stop to speak it ( )

TEST · 51

※下列各題，請依文意選出一個最適當的答案。

1. ______ can tell us what is happening in the world.
   (A) History
   (B) Math
   (C) Posters
   (D) Newspapers ( )

2. He never eats in this restaurant, and ______.
   (A) so do I
   (B) so I do
   (C) neither do I
   (D) neither I don't ( )

3. Rose ______ something firmly with both her hands on the icy sea.
   (A) held
   (B) founded
   (C) had
   (D) died ( )

4. Since it is so far from here, ______
   (A) starting to go there right now.
   (B) let's to ride our bicycles.
   (C) why not getting on the bus?
   (D) why not take the bus? ( )

5. The magazine cost you a lot of money, ______ it?
   (A) has
   (B) does
   (C) didn't
   (D) doesn't ( )

6. I make it a habit to listen to "Let's Talk in English" on the __________ every day.
   (A) radio
   (B) program
   (C) book
   (D) tree ( )

7. The math teacher is so __________ that every student is scared of him.
   (A) comfortable
   (B) frightened
   (C) strict
   (D) surprised ( )

8. Our rules and __________ may be different. But if they can make our class better, they are good.
   (A) ours
   (B) their
   (C) yours
   (D) your ( )

9. At this time of the year, the call of spring __________ sleeping bears up.
   (A) wakes
   (B) washes
   (C) shuts
   (D) locks ( )

10. Peter did not do well in math so he needed __________ harder.
   (A) studying
   (B) to study
   (C) to be studied
   (D) studies ( )

TEST · 52

※下列各題，請依文意選出一個最適當的答案。

1. We ________ to give Father a pair of sunglasses for Father's Day.
   (A) changed
   (B) became
   (C) decided
   (D) trained ( )

2. Necessity is the mother of ________.
   (A) vacation
   (B) invention
   (C) conversation
   (D) station ( )

3. It is ________ crying over spilt milk.
   (A) no way
   (B) no wonder
   (C) no use
   (D) not at all ( )

4. ________ this glass carefully; I don't want it broken.
   (A) Been held
   (B) To hold
   (C) Hold
   (D) Holding ( )

5. We've had no news from our daughter ________.
   (A) yet
   (B) ago
   (C) until
   (D) two days ( )

6. We cannot change our _________, but we can make our future different.
   (A) concentration
   (B) decoration
   (C) past
   (D) novel ( )

7. Mr. Brown got home too late last night and was _________ out by his wife.
   (A) locked
   (B) practiced
   (C) joined
   (D) worried ( )

8. English is used by 600 million people as the world _________ of business and science.
   (A) brake
   (B) blackboard
   (C) traffic
   (D) language ( )

9. Who _________ breakfast for you every day?
   (A) does make
   (B) cooking
   (C) makes
   (D) to make ( )

10. The MRT system makes transportation more convenient and _________.
   (A) comfortable
   (B) silly
   (C) dangerous
   (D) surprised ( )

TEST · 53

※下列各題，請依文意選出一個最適當的答案。

1. See ________ you can make an egg stand on Dragon Boat Festival.
(A) if
(B) when
(C) what
(D) which ( )

2. Believe me. This is the best story you ________.
(A) make up
(B) have ever made
(C) ever made
(D) have ever made up ( )

3. Do you know why she changed her ________?
(A) size
(B) pinball
(C) lap
(D) mind ( )

4. Summer is my favorite ________ of the year.
(A) month
(B) holiday
(C) instant
(D) season ( )

5. What's so ________ about the new video game?
(A) real
(B) hungry
(C) special
(D) worried ( )

6. If you feel bored by studying all day, you can go ________ for some fresh air.
   (A) outdoor
   (B) indoor
   (C) outside
   (D) outer space ( )

7. The doctor suggested Father quit smoking for his ________.
   (A) action
   (B) museum
   (C) practice
   (D) health ( )

8. Good learners ________ on their studies, and they are not afraid of asking questions.
   (A) charge
   (B) examine
   (C) concentrate
   (D) answer ( )

9. My husband likes reading but I like gardening. My husband and I like ________ things. We are not the same at all.
   (A) different
   (B) convenient
   (C) thick
   (D) heavy ( )

10. Traffic rules should be ________ by all pedestrians and drivers.
    (A) followed
    (B) burned
    (C) bumped
    (D) found ( )

pedestrian 行人

TEST · 54

※ 下列各題，請依文意選出一個最適當的答案。

1. Tom has studied English ________.
   (A) for a long time
   (B) some day
   (C) in the future
   (D) last month ( )

2. I want to try on the ________ blue dress.
   (A) minute
   (B) medium
   (C) color
   (D) moment ( )

3. If it ________ tomorrow, I will not go there.
   (A) rained
   (B) to rain
   (C) rains
   (D) will rain ( )

4. Only a(n) ________ student would try to cheat in tests.
   (A) national
   (B) healthy
   (C) stupid
   (D) angry ( )

5. In Taipei, people must pay for special garbage ________, which are a little expensive.
   (A) workers
   (B) food
   (C) bags
   (D) questions ( )

6. ________ pretty these roses are! It is nice of you to send me flowers.

(A) What
(B) That
(C) Which
(D) How ( )

7. Go ________ the street three blocks and you will see the bookstore.

(A) along
(B) alone
(C) long
(D) lonely ( )

8. Heavy traffic not only wastes people's time but also produces serious air ________.

(A) vacation
(B) pollution
(C) question
(D) decision ( )

9. It will do you good to eat rich food for ________, not for dinner.

(A) meal
(B) breakfast
(C) order
(D) menu ( )

10. He doesn't like Oolong tea, and his girlfriend doesn't, ________.

(A) neither
(B) nor
(C) too
(D) either ( )

TEST · 55

※ 下列各題，請依文意選出一個最適當的答案。

1. The school ________ I'm studying is quite near my house.
   (A) how
   (B) why
   (C) which
   (D) where ( )

2. The ________ work made me ________.
   (A) troubled ; worrying
   (B) changing ; surprising
   (C) excited ; satisfied
   (D) boring ; tired ( )

3. ________ usually has twenty-eight days, but it has twenty-nine days every four years.
   (A) December
   (B) September
   (C) January
   (D) February ( )

4. Cell phones have made ________ more convenient.
   (A) decoration
   (B) information
   (C) playground
   (D) communication ( )

5. I am better in ________ than in English.
   (A) factory
   (B) history
   (C) dictionary
   (D) library ( )

6. Mary came to Taiwan on __________ and she will stay here for two weeks.
   (A) program
   (B) interest
   (C) business
   (D) birthday ( )

7. Lisa is not popular with others because she likes to __________ people.
   (A) notice
   (B) criticize
   (C) watch
   (D) grade ( )

8. My teacher __________ me to do the exercise after school every day.
   (A) had
   (B) made
   (C) helped
   (D) talked ( )

9. I was in such a hurry that I parked my car in front of the hospital, though I knew it was __________.
   (A) safe
   (B) wrong
   (C) correct
   (D) right ( )

10. We are going to move into a new apartment, which is __________ my father's office.
   (A) near
   (B) after
   (C) ago
   (D) from ( )

TEST · 56

※下列各題，請依文意選出一個最適當的答案。

1. After the typhoon, there was no _________ or running water in many houses.
   (A) electricity
   (B) rain
   (C) right
   (D) aunt ( )

2. The dog _________ when someone knocked on the door.
   (A) packed
   (B) rang
   (C) barked
   (D) wasted ( )

3. They went to the park _________.
   (A) on bus
   (B) by buses
   (C) by a bus
   (D) by bus ( )

4. Don't cheat on exams, _________ you will be punished.
   (A) yet
   (B) but
   (C) and
   (D) or ( )

5. Carol _________ me that she had telephoned you yesterday.
   (A) said
   (B) told
   (C) spoke
   (D) talked ( )

6. When he saw the present, he was __________ glad __________ excited. He was angry.
   (A) more ; than
   (B) neither ; nor
   (C) either ; or
   (D) both ; and ( )

7. She just wanted to be __________. That's why she talked so loud.
   (A) fined
   (B) noticed
   (C) closed
   (D) worried ( )

8. Mr. Chen had __________ chickens and he made money by selling eggs.
   (A) two thousands
   (B) two thousands of
   (C) thousands of
   (D) thousands ( )

9. If the team had listened to the weather __________, they wouldn't have gone to climb the mountain.
   (A) joke
   (B) story
   (C) report
   (D) doctor ( )

10. She has the habit of __________ old letters and notes from her friends.
   (A) losing
   (B) hoping
   (C) keeping
   (D) using ( )

TEST · 57

※ 下列各題，請依文意選出一個最適當的答案。

1. David has a special ________ for painting. He paints very well.
   (A) fault
   (B) brand
   (C) talent
   (D) medicine ( )

2. I like movies, ________ action movies.
   (A) widely
   (B) hopelessly
   (C) separately
   (D) especially ( )

3. Tim spends more time ________ than ________.
   (A) study ; play
   (B) studying ; play
   (C) to study ; to play
   (D) studying ; playing ( )

4. Benz is a famous brand of ________ car.
   (A) experienced
   (B) excited
   (C) expensive
   (D) express ( )

5. May I have two ________, please?
   (A) coffee's cups
   (B) coffee cup
   (C) cup of coffees
   (D) cups of coffee ( )

6. I __________ the Wangs since I moved to the country in 1999.
   (A) know
   (B) have known
   (C) knew
   (D) will know ( )

7. The price of air conditioners __________ come down because winter is coming.
   (A) has been
   (B) has
   (C) had
   (D) have ( )

8. Koalas are found only in Australia. I think there is perhaps no cuter __________ than the koala.
   (A) plant
   (B) animal
   (C) hospital
   (D) people ( )

9. Of all the __________ of the past hundred years, TV has changed people's lives most.
   (A) shelves
   (B) sweater
   (C) notice
   (D) inventions ( )

10. There are four kinds of fruit on the table. You can __________ the one you like best.
   (A) sit
   (B) guess
   (C) make
   (D) take ( )

TEST · 58

※下列各題，請依文意選出一個最適當的答案。

1. He heard a dog ________ at the stranger in the garden.
   (A) barked
   (B) barking
   (C) to bark
   (D) barks ( )

2. Betty was pretty ________ when she first visited the National Palace Museum in Taiwan.
   (A) honest
   (B) avoid
   (C) impressed
   (D) afraid ( )

3. Where there is a will, ________ is a way.
   (A) it
   (B) which
   (C) where
   (D) there ( )

4. Don't judge a person by his ________.
   (A) address
   (B) calendar
   (C) looks
   (D) calculator ( )

5. I cannot find my ________. It must have been stolen.
   (A) wallet
   (B) style
   (C) waiter
   (D) wall ( )

6. A child usually goes to ________ school before he goes to junior high school.
   (A) elementary
   (B) exciting
   (C) electric
   (D) clerk ( )

7. The movie "Life is Beautiful," ________ the best foreign film, is quite interesting.
   (A) had also named
   (B) also naming
   (C) was also named
   (D) also named ( )

> 📖
> the best foreign film 最佳外語片

8. The ________ in Taiwan is very different from that in America.
   (A) window
   (B) weather
   (C) wherever
   (D) whether ( )

9. I am sorry that we should be made ________ so much work.
   (A) do
   (B) done
   (C) by doing
   (D) to do ( )

10. After playing basketball for two hours, I feel very ________.
   (A) thirsty
   (B) theater
   (C) teachable
   (D) tasty ( )

TEST · 59

※下列各題，請依文意選出一個最適當的答案。

1. Lisa usually wears a ________ smile on her face, so everybody likes to make friends with her.
   (A) old-fashioned
   (B) newest
   (C) friendly
   (D) impossible ( )

2. The ________ which I am reading now is fascinating.
   (A) cram
   (B) music
   (C) play
   (D) novel ( )

   fascinating 精彩

3. Don't be so ________ with him. After all, he is just a kid.
   (A) stamp
   (B) strict
   (C) study
   (D) surprise ( )

4. David is ________, but he is not the kind of boy I love.
   (A) tired
   (B) between
   (C) handsome
   (D) video ( )

5. Can you ________ life without music?
   (A) afford
   (B) finish
   (C) imagine
   (D) taste ( )

6. A : I'm not going to school this morning. It's English class and I hate verbs.

   B : ________

   (A) Neither do I
   (B) So do I
   (C) So am I
   (D) I am, too ( )

7. Today millions of people learn English ________ a foreign language.

   (A) by
   (B) for
   (C) under
   (D) as ( )

8. ________ to find a parking space near my office, so I go to work by MRT.

   (A) I'm impossible
   (B) It's impossible for me
   (C) It's impossible to me
   (D) It's impossible of me ( )

9. The ________ is ringing. Can you answer it, Tom?

   (A) homework
   (B) phone number
   (C) doorbell
   (D) animal ( )

10. ________ afraid of asking questions in class. The more you ask, the more you learn.

    (A) Not be
    (B) Be
    (C) Don't be
    (D) Not to be ( )

TEST · 60

※ 下列各題，請依文意選出一個最適當的答案。

1. ________, my English is getting better.
   (A) Because my teacher's help
   (B) Because of my hard work
   (C) Thanks to my teacher help me
   (D) Thanks to use good methods ( )

2. Most students don't like to have ________ every day.
   (A) tests
   (B) computer
   (C) theaters
   (D) movies ( )

3. Mother told me ________ tell a lie.
   (A) mustn't
   (B) had to
   (C) don't
   (D) not to ( )

4. It was dark, ________ I couldn't see what was happening.
   (A) so
   (B) but
   (C) because
   (D) or ( )

5. My neighbor's cat was very ________ last night. I couldn't sleep at all.
   (A) noisy
   (B) cute
   (C) delicious
   (D) lazily ( )

6. There are three students in the classroom. One of them is Tom. __________ are David and Jack.
   (A) Another
   (B) Some
   (C) Others
   (D) The others ( )

7. You will do things better and faster if you __________ more time working than complaining.
   (A) take
   (B) spend
   (C) cost
   (D) make ( )

📖 complain 抱怨

8. Richard and I are good friends, and both of us are basketball __________.
   (A) teams
   (B) skin
   (C) changes
   (D) fans ( )

9. A : Is Johnny going to be a taxi driver?
   B : No. He's really angry. They told him he is __________ the car.
   (A) so tall that he won't sit in
   (B) too tall that he will sit in
   (C) so tall that he might sit in
   (D) too tall to sit in ( )

10. Susan took five classes during the last __________.
   (A) unit
   (B) semester
   (C) office
   (D) underground ( )

TEST · 61

※下列各題，請依文意選出一個最適當的答案。

1. Exciting sports __________ by everyone, especially baseball and basketball.
   (A) is enjoyed
   (B) enjoy
   (C) are enjoying
   (D) are enjoyed ( )

2. In Taiwan, we usually have __________ in summer.
   (A) holidays
   (B) roof
   (C) typhoons
   (D) glasses ( )

3. The last month of the year is __________.
   (A) October
   (B) December
   (C) November
   (D) September ( )

4. The woman __________ is a doctor.
   (A) live next door
   (B) lives next door
   (C) who live next door
   (D) living next door ( )

5. After leaving school, I hope we'll stay in __________.
   (A) touch
   (B) village
   (C) software
   (D) active ( )

6. After dinner, I like to have some ________, such as ice cream or pudding.
   (A) desert
   (B) dessert
   (C) hamburgers
   (D) pizza ( )

7. Before entering the theater, you have to buy a movie ________.
   (A) poster
   (B) fan
   (C) dress
   (D) ticket ( )

8. A friendly smile helps us make ________ with others more easily.
   (A) friends
   (B) friend
   (C) a friend
   (D) friendly ( )

9. My classmates and I are going to ________ at the beach this weekend.
   (A) camp
   (B) shop
   (C) iron
   (D) drive ( )

10. They produced a new computer, ________ low price will make it very popular with students.
   (A) who
   (B) that
   (C) which
   (D) whose ( )

TEST · 62

※下列各題，請依文意選出一個最適當的答案。

1. My mother will go to England on business. Her ________ is next Monday.
   (A) church
   (B) date
   (C) flight
   (D) jeep ( )

2. There ________ a good movie on TV tonight.
   (A) will be
   (B) will have
   (C) will is
   (D) is going to have ( )

3. My sister is busy in the ________ preparing for an exam.
   (A) study
   (B) kitchen
   (C) bathroom
   (D) basement ( )

4. I can't find my backpack. Would you lend me ________?
   (A) you's
   (B) your
   (C) yous
   (D) yours ( )

5. Mark never looked happy at that time, ________?
   (A) isn't he
   (B) did he
   (C) didn't he
   (D) is he ( )

6. ________ have made our life more interesting and convenient.
   (A) Comic books
   (B) Computers
   (C) Hot springs
   (D) Medicine ( )

7. Christmas is coming. We'll ________ our classroom and have a party this Saturday.
   (A) draw
   (B) invite
   (C) enjoy
   (D) decorate ( )

8. If you want to send a letter, you need an ________ and a stamp.
   (A) envelope
   (B) eve
   (C) story
   (D) envelop ( )

9. He always asked me to let him ________ my math homework.
   (A) hire
   (B) copy
   (C) avoid
   (D) welcome ( )

10. If I ________ enough money yesterday, I would have bought the book.
   (A) had
   (B) have
   (C) had had
   (D) have had ( )

TEST · 63

※下列各題，請依文意選出一個最適當的答案。

1. "Do you know ________ it is?" "Yes, it's eight ten."
   (A) how old
   (B) how often
   (C) where
   (D) what time ( )

2. There is always ________ in the newspapers every day.
   (A) something surprising
   (B) some surprised things
   (C) surprising something
   (D) something surprised ( )

3. It's very ________ to tell John from Bill because they are twins.
   (A) different
   (B) weak
   (C) hand
   (D) difficult ( )

4. Tina's parents ________ her high grades in English.
   (A) are proud of
   (B) are interested in
   (C) are worried about
   (D) shut up ( )

5. Betty is ________ of the two girls.
   (A) taller
   (B) the taller
   (C) tallest
   (D) the tallest ( )

6. A ________ school is a place where students can keep studying after school.
   (A) rude
   (B) subway
   (C) free
   (D) cram ( )

7. Do you mind ________ the letter for me?
   (A) to mail
   (B) mailing
   (C) mailed
   (D) mail ( )

8. Many high school students work part-time in summer vacation so that they can earn their own money to buy ________ things.
   (A) welcome
   (B) active
   (C) fashionable
   (D) careful ( )

9. I always ________ my girlfriend when I ________ to work in Taipei.
   (A) think of ; go away
   (B) am thinking of ; went away
   (C) have thought of ; go away
   (D) was thinking of ; am going away ( )

10. We love ________ to the movies and do our homework together.
   (A) going
   (B) to go
   (C) go
   (D) gone ( )

TEST · 64

※ 下列各題，請依文意選出一個最適當的答案。

1. A new supermarket __________ next year.
   (A) was built
   (B) will going to build
   (C) is going to build
   (D) is going to be built ( )

2. Do what I tell you, __________.
   (A) so do I
   (B) why you do it
   (C) or you will be in trouble
   (D) that I will give you a present ( )

3. The driver told the __________ not to put their hands out of the windows.
   (A) passengers
   (B) visitors
   (C) waiters
   (D) learners ( )

4. This is the restaurant __________ we ate dinner.
   (A) in which
   (B) which
   (C) in where
   (D) there ( )

5. Pearl __________ stupid questions.
   (A) is always asking
   (B) always is asking
   (C) is asking all the time
   (D) is sometimes asking ( )

6. Jane __________ up in a happy family, and we like her very much.
   (A) excuse
   (B) grew
   (C) favorite
   (D) sigh ( )

7. In America, you can't buy medicine without your doctor's __________.
   (A) dictionary
   (B) prescription
   (C) mouth
   (D) relief ( )

8. There were many big earthquakes last month, and they really __________ us.
   (A) helped
   (B) scared
   (C) amused
   (D) excited ( )

📖 earthquake 地震

9. The driver __________ badly in this car accident.
   (A) hurted
   (B) was hurted
   (C) hurt
   (D) was hurt ( )

10. As the middle child of the three in her family, Laura often complains that her older brother and younger sister have taken almost all the love and care of their __________.
   (A) presidents
   (B) police
   (C) problems
   (D) parents ( )

TEST · 65

※下列各題，請依文意選出一個最適當的答案。

1. Certain products ________ must now work better and save more electricity.
   (A) are like lights and washing machines
   (B) we use in our homes
   (C) which affects modern living
   (D) so to fight pollution ( )

2. You have to go there, ________?
   (A) have you
   (B) haven't you
   (C) do you
   (D) don't you ( )

3. We study Japanese or English as a ________ language.
   (A) important
   (B) national
   (C) foreign
   (D) dead ( )

4. ________ is the weather ________ in Taipei in fall?
   (A) How ; like
   (B) What ; ×
   (C) What ; to be
   (D) What ; like ( )

5. To make students ________ in what they learn, many pictures are put in the books.
   (A) less interesting
   (B) more interesting
   (C) less interested
   (D) more interested ( )

6. George was not very smart. But he was _________ diligent of the two boys.
   (A) more
   (B) the more
   (C) most
   (D) the most ( )

7. Micky bought Nike sports shoes yesterday and the _________ was really low because of a special sale.
   (A) money
   (B) price
   (C) present
   (D) tale ( )

8. If an English _________ is long, you need to say it more carefully.
   (A) subject
   (B) novel
   (C) sentence
   (D) memory ( )

9. They say Sally Lin will teach us next year. So she is our _________ teacher.
   (A) future
   (B) changing
   (C) science
   (D) preview ( )

10. If there _________ a fire in this building, people will run out.
    (A) is
    (B) will be
    (C) were
    (D) has ( )

TEST · 66

※下列各題，請依文意選出一個最適當的答案。

1. Miss Wang is not __________. She catches a cold very easily.
   (A) welcome
   (B) strange
   (C) strong
   (D) busy ( )

2. When we meet people on the street, we usually say __________ to them.
   (A) happy
   (B) hello
   (C) thanks
   (D) nice ( )

3. The air in the country is __________ than that in the city.
   (A) fresher
   (B) more clear
   (C) more convenient
   (D) wider ( )

4. __________ English lessons __________ fun.
   (A) Learning ; are
   (B) Learn ; is
   (C) To learn ; are
   (D) To learn ; is ( )

5. You have to study harder, and __________ your friends.
   (A) so have
   (B) so does
   (C) neither do
   (D) so do ( )

6. The police stopped a man. They said he took some money from a store. They found the money in his wallet. So they took him to the ________.
   (A) hospital
   (B) police station
   (C) factory
   (D) home ( )

7. Do you know of any English word ________ from Chinese?
   (A) borrowing
   (B) borrow
   (C) borrowed
   (D) which borrowed ( )

8. There are lots of ________ in the night market that sell food, drinks, and clothes.
   (A) vacations
   (B) lives
   (C) vendors
   (D) villages ( )

9. The children are busy ________ presents for their mothers.
   (A) preparing
   (B) to prepare
   (C) prepared
   (D) prepare ( )

10. We sent flowers to the police officer ________ got hurt when he was trying to catch the thief.
   (A) who
   (B) whose
   (C) which
   (D) × ( )